Jeremy and the
Golden Fleece

Becky Citra
illustrated by Jessica Milne

ORCA BOOK PUBLISHERS

To my father
B.C.

To my loving mum
J.M.

Text copyright © 2007 Becky Citra
Illustrations copyright © 2007 Jessica Milne

Library and Archives Canada Cataloguing in Publication

Citra, Becky
Jeremy and the Golden Fleece / written by Becky Citra ; ill
Jessica Milne.
(Orca echoes)
ISBN 978-1-55143-657-9

I. Milne, Jessica, 1974- II. Title. III. Series.

PS8555.I87J473 2007 jC813'.54 C2006-907060-1

First published in the United States, 2007
Library of Congress Control Number: 2006939248

Summary: In this third book of the Jeremy and the Enchanted Theater series, Jeremy and
the cat, Aristotle, must travel into the Greek myth of *Jason and the Golden Fleece*,
face grave dangers and solve a riddle.

Orca Book Publishers gratefully acknowledges the support for its publishing programs
provided by the following agencies: the Government of Canada through the Book
Publishing Industry Development Program and the Canada Council for the Arts, and the
Province of British Columbia through the BC Arts Council
and the Book Publishing Tax Credit.

Typesetting by Christine Toller
Cover artwork and interior illustrations by Jessica Milne

ORCA BOOK PUBLISHERS
PO Box 5626, STN. B
VICTORIA, BC CANADA
V8R 6S4

ORCA BOOK PUBLISHERS
PO Box 468
CUSTER, WA USA
98240-0468

www.orcabook.com
Printed and bound in Canada.
Printed on 100% PCW recycled paper.
10 09 08 07 • 4 3 2 1

How the Adventure Began…

Long ago, the Enchanted Theater was a wonderful place. People came from everywhere to see the ancient Greek plays.

Then Mr. Magnus bought the theater. That's when the trouble started. Mr. Magnus made up new endings for the plays. He mixed up all the characters.

Zeus, the king of the Greek gods, was furious. He hurled lightning bolts at the theater. The power went out. People stopped coming to see the plays. The actors quit.

Jeremy and Aristotle the cat traveled back in time to meet Zeus. They traveled all the way to Mount Olympus, the home of the Greek gods.

Zeus told them that Mr. Magnus was ruining the Greek plays. He gave Jeremy three scrolls. Each scroll had a riddle. If Mr. Magnus solved all three riddles, Zeus promised that he would stop punishing the Enchanted Theater.

Mr. Magnus needed help from his friends. Jeremy and Aristotle traveled back in time to the ancient Greek underworld. They solved the first riddle.

Now they are ready for the second riddle!

Chapter One
The Enchanted Theater

Jeremy raced all the way to the Enchanted Theater.

Mr. Magnus and Aristotle the cat were waiting for him. They were in the little room at the end of the long dark hallway.

The room was filled with racks of bright costumes. Shields and swords gleamed in the corners.

Aristotle sat on top of a blue and gold trunk. Mr. Magnus perched on his stool by the window. Wobbly piles of books surrounded him. He was holding an ancient parchment scroll.

"The second riddle!" said Jeremy.

Jeremy was good at riddles. But Mr. Magnus looked worried.

"This is a tough one," he moaned. He opened the scroll and read out loud: "*I have twenty legs but just one wing. The sea is my kingdom and Jason my king. Who am I?*"

Jeremy frowned. "Twenty legs...one wing...," he mumbled. He screwed up his face. He thought as hard as he could.

"It's no use," sighed Mr. Magnus.

"We can't give up!" said Jeremy. "We have to save the Enchanted Theater!"

He looked over Mr. Magnus's shoulder. He studied the second riddle. "Jason my king," he said. "Who's Jason?"

"A Greek sailor," said Mr. Magnus.

Mr. Magnus picked up a book from the top of a pile. He opened it to a page in the middle. There was a picture of a large ship with a billowing sail.

The word *Argo* was painted boldly on the side of the ship.

A man stood at the bow. He gazed over the blue waves. His face was strong and proud.

"That's Jason," said Mr. Magnus.

"He's not just a sailor," said Jeremy. "He looks like the captain."

"It would help if you had seen the play," said Mr. Magnus. "It was a great success…until Zeus put out the lights. It's called *Jason and the Golden Fleece*."

"What's a fleece?" said Jeremy.

"It's the wooly hide from a sheep," said Mr. Magnus.

Jeremy shivered. A golden sheep sounded magical.

He made up his mind quickly. "We'll travel back in time again!" he said. "We'll find Jason. We'll ask him to help us solve the riddle."

Aristotle leaped off the blue and gold trunk. "Meow," he said.

"I need the backpack," said Jeremy.

Mr. Magnus picked up a bulging backpack. He handed it to Jeremy. Jeremy slid it over his shoulders.

"I hope you remember the rules," said Mr. Magnus.

Jeremy said the rules quickly in his head.

1. Time travel only happens at sunset.

2. You have to hold onto an actor's prop.

3. You have to do five brave things to return.

He looked at the pink sky that glowed through the one small window.

"We'd better hurry!" he said.

"But I haven't told you about the clashing rocks or the fire breathing bull or the serpent who never closes his eyes!" cried Mr. Magnus.

"Where's the prop!" said Jeremy.

Mr. Magnus hopped about nervously. He picked up a gleaming shield. "Jason's actor used this in a battle," he said.

Aristotle jumped onto Jeremy's shoulder.

Jeremy took a big breath. "We're ready!" he cried. He reached out and touched the shield.

Everything swirled around him.

From far away, he heard Mr. Magnus cry, "I've given you a map. You can use it to find Jason. And watch out for—"

Aristotle nudged Jeremy's cheek. And then everything went black.

Chapter Two
The *Argo*!

Jeremy opened his eyes.

He was standing on a dock in a busy harbor. Aristotle sat beside him, licking his ruffled orange fur.

The blue ocean sparkled in the sun. Ships with flapping sails bobbed up and down at the side of the dock.

Jeremy hunched his shoulders. "It sure is windy!" he said.

"A perfect day for sailing," said Aristotle.

"Look out, boy!" A sailor rolled a wooden barrel past him.

Jeremy leaped out of the way.

Men carried bundles and boxes to the ships. Loud

voices bellowed orders. Everyone was getting ready to leave. Jeremy's heart thumped. If he didn't find the *Argo* soon, it would be too late!

"Come on!" he said. "We have to find the *Argo* and talk to Jason!"

Jeremy pushed his way through the crowd. Aristotle darted at his side. Jeremy read the names painted on the sides of the ships.

Dragon, Wind Rider, Athena's Pride...

His heart beat faster. What if the *Argo* had already left?

Then he spotted it.

The *Argo* was at the end of the row of ships. It was the biggest and most graceful ship of them all.

Jeremy watched sailors roll barrels of supplies up the wooden plank onto the ship.

"Those sailors are called Argonauts," said Aristotle. "Jason picked them specially to be his crew. It was in the play at the Enchanted Theater."

"Argonauts sounds like astronauts," said Jeremy. It would be so cool to be an Argonaut.

Well, why not?

He remembered the backpack. It had helped him before. He slid it off his shoulders and unzipped it. He dug inside.

Jeremy pulled out a strange assortment of objects. He found a roll of paper, a long skinny stick that looked like a firecracker, a slingshot and a small round mirror. From the very bottom of the pack he dug out a folded piece of cloth.

Jeremy put everything back except the cloth. He unfolded it. It was a tunic, just like the one Jason was wearing in Mr. Magnus's book. Wrapped inside was a pair of leather sandals.

Jeremy pulled the tunic over his T-shirt and shorts. He took off his runners and put on the sandals.

Now he looked just like an Argonaut.

"It's now or never!" cried Jeremy.

13

Aristotle flicked his tail. He jumped on Jeremy's shoulder.

Jeremy took in a deep breath. He stepped behind one of the Argonauts and stared straight ahead. He followed the Argonaut up the wooden plank.

Jeremy let the breath out.

He was on board the *Argo*!

Chapter Three
Cast Off!

The Argonauts worked hard. They stowed away the barrels of supplies. They coiled up long ropes. They checked the sail. Nobody looked at Jeremy.

Aristotle had disappeared.

"Um…excuse me," said Jeremy. "Does anyone know where Jason is?"

Whoosh!

A fierce gust of wind tore at the sail. The ropes tied to the dock creaked and groaned.

The Argonauts sat down on the benches beside the long wooden oars.

Jeremy's heart thudded. The *Argo* was ready to leave. He had to find Jason.

Jeremy hurried to the bow of the ship. He gazed out at the blue waves.

Just for a second, he felt like Jason in the picture in Magnus's book. He felt strong and brave. He felt like a captain.

"ALL HANDS ON DECK!" yelled Jeremy. "HEAVE TO!"

The *Argo* strained at its ropes. Waves splashed the bow. Jeremy shivered. If the *Argo* were his, he would sail around the world!

"CAST OFF!" he hollered.

Ropes sang. The sail filled. Oars splashed. The *Argo* bounded over the blue water.

Jeremy spun around. "Wait!" he cried. "I was just kidding!"

The Argonauts stopped rowing. Their mouths dropped open.

"Hey, you're not Jason!" cried a big burly Argonaut.

"What do you think you're doing?" cried another.

"Yeah," demanded a third. "Where's Jason?"

"Er…over there," hissed a voice beside Jeremy.

Aristotle squeezed out from behind a coil of rope. He twitched his tail and stared at the shore.

Jeremy stared too.

A young man raced down the dock. He wore a tunic just like Jeremy's. His face was purple.

The man waved his fist.

Jeremy gulped.

He had seen that man before in Mr. Magnus's book.

It was Jason!

Chapter Four
Aristotle's Plan

"GO BACK!" shouted Jeremy. "TURN THE SHIP AROUND!"

"We can't," said an Argonaut.

"The wind is blowing the wrong way," grunted another.

"We're going to get in big trouble now," groaned a third.

Jeremy stared at the shore. Jason stood at the end of the dock. He cupped his hands to his mouth. He hollered something.

"I think he said, 'Bring my ship back!'" said Aristotle.

"Great, just great," said Jeremy. "He'll never help us solve the riddle now."

The *Argo* sped across the water. Jeremy watched Jason until he was just a tiny speck. And then he was gone.

"Now what do we do?" said Jeremy.

"Easy," said Aristotle. "We keep going and get the Golden Fleece."

The Argonauts stopped grumbling among themselves and listened. Jeremy listened too.

"I saw the play at the Enchanted Theater," said Aristotle. "The King of Colchis stole the Golden Fleece from Jason's uncle, King Pelias. If Jason gets the fleece back, his uncle said that he can be king. That's why Jason built the *Argo*!"

Jeremy said slowly, "If we sail to Colchis and get the Golden Fleece…"

"And give it to Jason…," said the big burly Argonaut.

"And Jason gets to be king…," added Aristotle.

"He won't be mad at us anymore!" finished Jeremy. "And he'll help us solve the riddle!"

Jeremy remembered something. He reached into the

backpack and took out the rolled-up piece of paper. He spread it out on the deck. The paper was covered with pictures and words in Mr. Magnus's spidery printing.

The Argonauts peered over his shoulder.

"A map!" they cried. "A map to Colchis and the Golden Fleece!"

They stared at Jeremy.

The big burly Argonaut stepped forward. "I'm Marco," he said, "your first mate."

Jeremy shook his hand. "I'm Jeremy." He stood up tall. "Your new captain."

Screech!

Everyone gazed up at the sky.

Three huge black vultures streaked toward the ship.

"The Harpies!" yelled Aristotle. "They were in the play."

"Duck!" shouted Jeremy.

But Aristotle had already disappeared inside an empty barrel.

Chapter Five
The Harpies

The black birds swooped toward the *Argo*. Their screams made Jeremy's back prickle.

Their enormous wings blocked the sun.

"Yikes!" cried the Argonauts. They pushed and shoved each other. They squeezed under the benches.

Jeremy crawled under a bench too.

He held his breath.

Claws scrabbled on the wooden deck. Wings flapped. A bird screeched. The ship rocked back and forth.

What was happening?

Then everything was still.

Jeremy crawled back out. After all, he was the captain of the *Argo*!

He looked up. The Harpies had left. But they were circling above the ship. They were coming back!

This time Jeremy didn't hide. He grabbed his backpack. He pulled out the skinny stick. A piece of cord hung out of one end. Tiny writing on the side said *Ship's Flare*.

Jeremy wasn't sure what a flare was. But the stick looked like the biggest firecracker he had ever seen!

He held the stick high in the air.

"One!" he shouted.

The Harpies streaked toward the ship.

"Two!" cried Jeremy.

The Harpies were so close he could feel the wind from their wings. He gasped. They had faces like old hags with stringy gray hair and wrinkled cheeks.

"Three!" he shouted.

He pulled the cord.

A blinding red light shot out the end like a rocket. It was brighter than a thousand firecrackers. It lit up the sky with a fiery glow.

"Wow!" said Jeremy. He hunched his shoulders. He closed his eyes.

The Harpies screamed. Their huge wings beat the air.

Jeremy shuddered. He waited a minute. Then he opened his eyes. A black feather drifted down from the blue sky. The Harpies were small dots in the distance.

"It's safe to come out!" shouted Jeremy.

The Argonauts crawled out from under the benches. Aristotle scrambled out of the barrel. He leaped onto the ship railing. The Argonauts laughed and cheered. "Hooray for Jeremy!"

Jeremy strode to the bow of the ship. His heart jumped. The *Argo* was skimming toward a rocky beach.

Faster and faster the wind blew the ship.

"We're going to crash!" shouted Jeremy.

Rocks smashed against the ship's hull. The Argonauts toppled like bowling pins. Jeremy slid across the deck.

"Aristotle!" he yelled. With a desperate yowl, Aristotle tumbled over the side of the ship.

Chapter Six
The Shipbuilder

Jeremy ran to the railing. He peered over the side. The *Argo* was sitting in shallow water. The bow rested on a rocky beach.

Aristotle was gone.

"Put down the gangplank!" said Jeremy.

Marco and two other Argonauts lowered the gangplank. Jeremy sped onto the beach.

A thin wet orange rat crawled out of the water. Jeremy blinked. The rat mewed crossly. It was Aristotle!

"I want to go home," he hissed.

"But we haven't solved the riddle," said Jeremy.

"Ahoy there! Ahoy there!" someone shouted.

At the end of the beach, a man waved a stick.

"Ahoy!" shouted Jeremy.

The man hobbled across the rocks to the *Argo*. He had a long gray beard. He was the oldest man Jeremy had ever seen.

"I saw the whole thing!" the man panted. He held out his hand. "I'm Phineus. Best shipbuilder on the island."

"Wow," said Jeremy.

Phineus slapped his leg. "That's because my wife Hester and I are the only ones who live here!"

Jeremy laughed. "I'm Jeremy," he said, "captain of the *Argo*."

He looked at the ship. It was leaning to one side. "And we sure need a shipbuilder."

Phineus's eyes sparkled. "I haven't had a ship to work on for thirty years!"

Jeremy thought Phineus looked too old to fix anything. "I can't pay you," he said.

"You got rid of the Harpies!" said Phineus. "They've

been after us as long as we've lived here. Stealing our food! Screeching night and day! Giving us no peace!"

Jeremy looked at the clear blue sky. "I don't think they'll be coming back."

"Then let's get started!" said Phineus.

Jeremy and the Argonauts helped. Hammers banged. Saws whirred. Phineus hopped about on his thin legs, checking the work.

In no time at all, the *Argo* was upright. It floated proudly on the blue water.

It was time to go. Jeremy looked around for Aristotle. He was nowhere in sight.

"You can't leave yet," said Phineus. "You have to meet Hester."

Phineus and Jeremy walked to a hut at the end of the beach. It was made out of driftwood. It had round windows and a driftwood deck.

"It looks like a ship!" said Jeremy. "It's wonderful."

He ducked through the low doorway. He looked

around. It was like a ship inside too. There were two bunks and a driftwood table and chairs. Sunlight shone through the round windows.

Hester rocked back and forth in a chair made of sticks. She looked even older than Phineus.

Aristotle sat on the floor beside an empty plate. He licked his whiskers. Jeremy could smell fish.

"So there you are!" he said.

"We've become friends," said Hester. Aristotle purred.

Jeremy thought Hester looked very wise.

"Have you ever seen anything with twenty legs and one wing?" he said.

Hester frowned. Then she shook her head.

"It's a riddle," sighed Jeremy. "We better go. We have to find King Colchis and get the Golden Fleece back."

Hester stood up. She reached for a small clay jar on a shelf. She handed it to Jeremy. "A gift for the brave captain who saved us from the Harpies," she said.

The jar smelled sweet and smoky. "What's it for?" said Jeremy.

"You'll know when the time comes," said Hester.

Jeremy put the jar in his backpack. "Come on, Aristotle," he said.

Outside the hut, the wind was blowing hard again. Phineus walked back with Jeremy to the *Argo*. Aristotle rode on Jeremy's shoulder.

When they got to the ship, Phineus clutched Jeremy's arm. "I have to warn you about the Clashing Rocks!"

It was hard to hear Phineus over the howling wind. The sail on the *Argo* flapped loudly.

"It looks like we're ready to go!" said Jeremy.

Phineus gripped his arm harder. "Two tall rocks on each side of the sea. They crash together when a ship sails between them. The only way to get through is…"

Marco leaned over the railing. "The wind's getting too strong!" he shouted.

Aristotle jumped off Jeremy's shoulder. He scampered up the gangplank.

"Good-bye!" said Jeremy. "And thank you!"

He pulled away from Phineus. He ran after Aristotle.

Marco pulled up the gangplank. The *Argo* sailed away.

Jeremy looked back at the island. Phineus stood on the rocky beach. He waved his stick in the air. Jeremy waved back.

Chapter Seven
The Clashing Rocks

The *Argo* sailed on. Jeremy got the map out of the backpack. He spread it on the deck.

"There's the harbor where we started," he said. "And there's Phineus and Hester's island!"

Jeremy peered more closely at the map. Mr. Magnus had drawn two pointed rocks. There was a narrow strip of water in between.

"We're almost at the Clashing Rocks," he shouted. "They don't look so bad! No problem!"

Jeremy looked up from the map.

Two huge spires of black rock rose right in front of the ship. Waves smashed against them. Foam sprayed high above the *Argo*'s mast.

The Argonauts froze.

"ROW BACKWARD!" shouted Jeremy.

The Argonauts heaved on their oars. The *Argo* bucked up and down in the waves.

Jeremy stared at the jagged rocks. He shivered. A piece of a ship's mast bobbed up and down in the foaming water.

What had Phineus said?

They crash together when a ship sails between them. The only way to get through is to…

Jeremy groaned. If only he had listened!

"What should we do, Captain?" said Marco. "The men can't hold the ship back much longer."

Jeremy stared at Aristotle. "You saw the play at the Enchanted Theater. How did Jason get past the Clashing Rocks?"

"Er…I was chasing a mouse in that part," mumbled Aristotle, "but it had something to do with a bird."

Jeremy thought hard.

"I bet I know!" he said. "We have to trick the Clashing

Rocks. If we send a bird ahead of us, the rocks will smash together. And then when they open again, we can sneak through fast!"

"We don't have a bird," said Aristotle.

"But we do have a slingshot!" cried Jeremy.

He dug the slingshot out of the backpack.

Marco gave him a hard round apple from a barrel.

Jeremy stood in the bow of the ship.

"ONE!" said Jeremy.

He pulled the rubber sling back as far as he could.

"TWO!"

The Argonauts leaned over the oars.

"THREE!"

Jeremy let go of the sling. The apple flew through the air. It soared right between the Clashing Rocks.

The jagged black rocks smashed together with a thundering crash. Jeremy's ears rang.

Then Jeremy and the crew watched the rocks move slowly apart.

"NOW!" shouted Jeremy. "ROW FOR YOUR LIVES!"

The *Argo* flew through the narrow strip of water.

The huge rocks loomed over the ship. Waves smashed against the hull. Icy air blasted them.

Then the warm sun shone on Jeremy's face. The sea was smooth and blue. They had left the Clashing Rocks behind.

The Argonauts cheered.

But Jeremy didn't cheer. The *Argo* sped past a little bay toward a high steep cliff. On top of the cliff stood a magnificent golden palace.

Three guards paced back and forth along the edge of the cliff.

Jeremy gulped. They had reached the home of King Colchis.

Chapter Eight
King Colchis

When they got closer, Jeremy could hear the guards.

"HUP! HUP! HUP!" they shouted.

The guards stared straight ahead. They marched back and forth along the cliff.

"HUP! HUP! HUP!"

Jeremy gazed up at the palace. High in a tower window something shiny glinted.

A spyglass! thought Jeremy. Someone was watching them.

"Go back to that bay!" he ordered.

The Argonauts rowed into the little bay. There was no wind. They pulled in the oars. The ship drifted close to a narrow strip of beach.

"I'm going ashore," said Jeremy.

Aristotle slunk behind the apple barrel.

"And you're coming with me," he added.

Marco lowered a rope ladder. Jeremy put on his backpack. He climbed down the ladder. He waded onto the beach.

Aristotle jumped off the ship's railing. He landed with a thump beside Jeremy.

The Argonauts leaned over the railing. "Good luck!" they called.

Jeremy and Aristotle walked along the beach. They walked until they were at the bottom of the steep cliff.

"HUP! HUP! HUP!" chanted the guards high above them.

Narrow steps were cut into the cliff. They zigzagged back and forth.

"Follow me," said Jeremy.

Up and up Jeremy and Aristotle climbed.

"HUP! HUP! HUP!"

"They're too busy marching," whispered Jeremy. "They don't know we're here."

"HUP! HUP! HUP!"

He stuck his head over the top of the cliff. He stared into two cold gray eyes. Above the eyes glittered a golden crown.

King Colchis!

Aristotle stuck his head over Jeremy's shoulder.

"Some guards," he said loudly. "A pussycat could break into this place. Get it? A..."

King Colchis grabbed Jeremy with one hand. He grabbed Aristotle with the other.

The king's yellow hair flowed to his shoulders. His crown sparkled in the sun.

Jeremy took a big breath.

"Pleased to meet you, your majesty," he said. "I'm Jeremy, captain of the *Argo*."

Chapter Nine
The Fire-Breathing Bull

"Jason." King Colchis's smile made Jeremy shiver. "I was wondering when you would get here."

"Uh…it's Jeremy," said Jeremy.

"Jason…Jeremy…whatever." The icy smile changed to a scowl. "You've come for my golden fleece."

Aristotle jumped on Jeremy's shoulder. "Remember Uncle Pelias," he whispered in his ear.

"Uh…the Golden Fleece belongs to Uncle Pelias," said Jeremy. "I mean, he's not *my* uncle."

King Colchis snapped his fingers. The guards stopped marching. They hurried to his side.

"Jason has come for the Golden Fleece," said King Colchis. "And he brought his cat to help him!"

The guards laughed. Aristotle's fur bristled.

"I'M JEREMY," shouted Jeremy.

King Colchis snapped his fingers again. The guards stopped laughing.

He peered more closely at Jeremy. "Isn't Jason supposed to be some kind of hero?"

He turned to the guards. "Does he look like a hero to you?"

Jeremy sighed. He was going to say "I'm Jeremy!" again, but it was no use.

The king smiled his icy smile. "So you think you're a hero—"

"I don't," said Jeremy.

"...who's going to take the Golden Fleece back to his uncle."

"Not *my* uncle," said Jeremy wearily.

"Then prove it!" snapped King Colchis.

Jeremy was all mixed up. "Prove what?" he stammered.

"That you're a hero."

King Colchis winked at the guards. "Take…whatever his name is…to the bull. It's time for our hero to have a little ride."

A guard grabbed Jeremy's left arm. Another guard grabbed his right arm. The third guard prodded Jeremy's back.

King Colchis led the way. The guards and Jeremy followed.

Aristotle rode on Jeremy's shoulder. "This isn't good," he muttered. "Do you remember what Mr. Magnus said about the bull?"

Jeremy shook his head.

"Fire breathing," hissed Aristotle. "That's what he said. FIRE-BREATHING BULL."

"There's no such a thing as a fire-breathing bull," said Jeremy. "I mean, there are fire-breathing dragons, but whoever heard of a—"

Jeremy came to a dead stop. His mouth dropped open.

Tied to a stake beside the palace was an enormous bull.

The bull pawed the ground, sending up clouds of dust. It turned and looked at Jeremy and the guards with its small red eyes. It let out a roar of rage.

Jeremy's legs turned to jelly as a fiery blast of orange and red flames shot out of the bull's mouth.

Chapter Ten
The Magic Ointment

"Don't do it," said Aristotle.

"I have to," said Jeremy. "If I don't ride the bull, King Colchis won't give me the Golden Fleece. And Jason will stay mad, and we'll never solve the riddle!"

"Ready for some fun?" said the king. He glared at the guards who were creeping away. "Get the meat!"

One of the guards scurried into the palace.

Jeremy slid his backpack off his shoulders. He glanced at the king.

King Colchis was pacing back and forth.

The bull bellowed. He sent out another blast of fire.

Jeremy opened his backpack.

He remembered Hester's gentle voice. *You'll know when the time comes.*

Jeremy took out the clay jar. He opened it. It was filled with ointment.

It didn't smell like something to eat. Quickly he rubbed the ointment on his arms and face.

The guard came back with a chunk of red meat. He tossed it to the pawing bull.

"Do it now, you fools!" cried the king. "While the bull's not looking!"

The other guards grabbed Jeremy. They dragged him to the bull. They slung him onto its back.

The bull lifted its huge head. It bucked hard. The rope tied to the stake snapped.

Jeremy shot up in the air. He landed with a thump.

The bull gave an enormous snort.

Jeremy grabbed the thick hair on the bull's neck.

The bull spun in a circle. It bucked and blew fire. Up and down, back and forth bounced Jeremy.

The bull charged past King Colchis and Aristotle and the three guards. It raced around the back of the palace.

"HEEELP!" yelled Jeremy. He closed his eyes.

A deep voice said, "So where do you want to go?"

Jeremy opened his eyes. "Huh?" he said. "You can talk?"

"First time," said the bull. It sounded surprised too.

Hester's ointment, thought Jeremy. It was magic!

"Do you know where King Colchis keeps the Golden Fleece?" he said quickly.

"Sure, but I don't think you want to—"

"I do!" said Jeremy. "And would you mind turning off that fire?"

They ran right around the palace. They flew past King Colchis and the guards.

"Jump on, Aristotle!" Jeremy yelled.

Aristotle sprang onto the bull's back. The guards gaped. The king's mouth dropped open.

Jeremy laughed. He felt like he was flying.

"Take us to the Golden Fleece!" he cried.

Chapter Eleven
The Golden Fleece

The bull ran and ran.

It stopped at the edge of a dark forest. "I'll wait for you here," it said. "And don't say I didn't warn you!"

Jeremy and Aristotle slid off its back.

They walked into the forest. The trees were close together. No birds sang.

Suddenly the trees ended. The sun shone into a grassy clearing.

"There it is!" said Jeremy.

In the middle of the clearing was a huge tree. The Golden Fleece hung from a thick branch. It glimmered in the sun.

Jeremy stared harder. The branch was red with orange spots. Sharp spines stuck out along the top.

"I never saw a—," began Jeremy.

The branch moved. Two huge golden eyes stared at them.

Jeremy and Aristotle jumped back.

"The serpent that never closes its eyes!" said Aristotle. "Er...I better check on the bull."

Jeremy grabbed Aristotle's tail.

Aristotle sighed. "You got anything left in that backpack?"

Jeremy looked inside the backpack. He pulled out the small round mirror. He tipped it back and forth. The sun winked off its surface.

Aristotle blinked hard. "Hey!" he cried. "Don't shine that thing in my face!"

Aristotle and Jeremy looked at each other. Then they looked at the serpent's huge golden eyes.

"I'll hold the mirror," said Jeremy, "and you grab—"

"How about *I* hold the mirror and *you*—"

"Okay, okay," said Jeremy. He propped the mirror

against Aristotle's paw. He tilted it at the sun. A beam of bright light bounced off the mirror straight to the tree.

The serpent snapped its huge eyes shut. Its spiny tail lashed back and forth.

"Now or never," muttered Jeremy.

He ran to the tree. He jumped up and grabbed the Golden Fleece.

"Got it!" he cried.

Jeremy slung the fleece over his shoulder. He and Aristotle sped out of the clearing.

Jeremy looked back once. The serpent hissed and flashed its sharp fangs. Its golden eyes gleamed with rage.

Jeremy and Aristotle ran through the dark forest. They jumped on the waiting bull's back.

"Back to the *Argo*!" cried Jeremy.

The bull raced to the edge of the high cliff. Jeremy and Aristotle scrambled off.

"Will you get in trouble?" said Jeremy.

The bull pawed the ground and snorted. It opened his mouth. Jeremy felt a blast of fiery air.

Hester's magic had worn off!

"Good-bye," said Jeremy quickly, "and thank you!"

The bull gave a huge buck and galloped away. Jeremy looked down at the blue bay. The wind had picked up. The *Argo's* sail billowed. The Argonauts sat on the benches, their oars ready.

Jeremy stared harder. "It's the *Argo*!" he cried.

"Of course it's the *Argo*," muttered Aristotle. "What did you—"

"The riddle!" said Jeremy. "I have twenty legs and just one wing. It's the *Argo*! The sail is the wing and the oars are the legs."

"Now we can go home!" said Aristotle.

"Don't forget the *Enchanted Theater Rule Book*," said Jeremy. "I have to do five brave things to return home."

"You chased away the Harpies," said Aristotle. "That's one."

"And I sailed through the Clashing Rocks," added Jeremy. "That's two."

"You tamed the fire-breathing bull!" said Aristotle. "That's three!"

"I stole the Golden Fleece from the serpent who never closes its eyes," said Jeremy. "That's four!"

Just then there was a loud rumble. The ground shook. Jeremy and Aristotle looked back.

King Colchis and his guards streamed out of the palace gates. But this time there weren't three guards. There were hundreds. All mounted on swift black horses.

"Run!" yelled Aristotle.

Chapter Twelve
Back Home

Jeremy and Aristotle ran back to the steps in the cliff. They scrambled down and raced along the beach.

"Hurry!" yelled Marco.

Aristotle jumped onto Jeremy's shoulder. Jeremy splashed through the water to the ladder. Up he climbed.

"Close call, Captain," said Marco.

Jeremy looked back. King Colchis and his guards lined the edge of the cliff. King Colchis shouted something. He jumped up and down.

"Sorry!" Jeremy yelled. "Can't stay!"

The Argonauts crowded around Jeremy and the Golden Fleece. Then Jeremy strode to the bow of the ship.

"ALL HANDS ON DECK!" he shouted. "HEAVE TO! CAST OFF!"

The *Argo* bounded over the waves. King Colchis and his guards were left far behind.

The wind blew in Jeremy's face. He was the captain of the *Argo*!

And then he froze.

Around the tip of the bay raced a sailing ship. It had two sails and rows and rows of oars. It flew straight toward them.

A man stood in the bow.

Jeremy gulped. It was Jason!

The Argonauts saw the ship too. "Should we try to outrun them?" called Marco.

Jeremy took a big breath. "No," he said. "Pull in the oars."

The huge ship sailed right up to the *Argo*.

Jeremy swallowed. "Ahoy!" he said.

"Ahoy!" said Jason.

Jeremy held up the Golden Fleece. "Are you looking for this?"

Jason laughed. It was a huge joyful laugh that rocked both ships.

Aristotle jumped onto Jeremy's shoulder.

"The fifth brave thing!" he whispered. "You didn't run away from Jason!"

Jeremy was just thinking that he would like to have the sailor with the big laugh for a friend.

And everything went black.

"You made it!" said Mr. Magnus.

Jeremy looked around. He was in the little room in the Enchanted Theater. Aristotle sat on top of the blue and gold trunk.

Mr. Magnus peered at Jeremy through his round glasses.

"I sailed the *Argo!*" said Jeremy. "I chased away the Harpies, and I made it through the Clashing Rocks, and I rode the bull and—"

Aristotle twitched his tail.

"Aristotle helped," added Jeremy quickly. "He's the bravest cat in the whole world!"

"But did you solve the riddle?" said Mr. Magnus.

He waved the scroll. He read in a trembling voice: "*I have twenty legs but just one wing. The sea is my kingdom and Jason my king.*"

"It's the *Argo*!" cried Jeremy. "The sail is the wing and the oars are the legs!"

A lightning bolt that leaned against the wall lit up with a dazzling glow.

Mr. Magnus nodded with satisfaction. "Zeus's lightning bolt. That means you got the right answer."

He shook Jeremy's hand. "Now, my boy, it's time for you to go home for supper."

Jeremy waved good-bye at the door. "I'll be back tomorrow to help solve the last riddle," he promised.

"Good-bye! Good-bye!" said Mr. Magnus.

"Meow," said Aristotle.

Becky Citra is also the author of the Max and Ellie books, Orca Young Readers set in Upper Canada. She lives in Bridge Lake, British Columbia.

Jeremy and the Golden Fleece is Book 3 in the Jeremy series following *Jeremy and the Enchanted Theater* and *Jeremy in the Underworld*. Watch for *Jeremy and the Fantastic Flying Machine* in 2008.

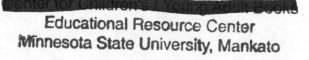